William Carnie

Waifs of Rhyme

William Carnie

Waifs of Rhyme

ISBN/EAN: 9783337259860

Printed in Europe, USA, Canada, Australia, Japan

Cover: Foto ©Andreas Hilbeck / pixelio.de

More available books at **www.hansebooks.com**

WAIFS OF RHYME

Rolling in his mind
Old Waifs of · Rhyme
Tennyson's "Brook"

ABERDEEN
LEWIS SMITH & SON
1890

ANOTHER WORD.

The present edition of WAIFS OF RHYME *is the outcome of requests by friends in humble life,—the life which the Author, through various causes, knows best.*

When the RHYMES *came from the Printer's hands, in 1887, they were intended solely for private circulation,—as indicated in the Prefatory Couplets, repeated here,—the prevailing motive of Publication at all being the acknowledged impatience of the writer in making copies of this and that special* WAIF. *The private circulation design was overruled by voices to which there was grateful reason the Author should listen, with the result that the booklet got, in Publisher's phrase, out of print in a couple of days, and can now, it appears, be only obtained, at a somewhat prohibitive price. Hence, and with the above opening explanation, this new issue.*

The first edition of the WAIFS *had an introductory, "One Word." In now prefixing* ANOTHER WORD, *the Author desires to repeat that there must be scores of things of like character from the same pen floating about here and there, but as they took form through momentary promptings, so they, apparently, found no abiding place in print. At any rate they are not at command. It may be noted, however, that the pieces here included from Page 63 are additions to the original collection.*

If these wandering WAIFS OF RHYME *afford some amusement to folks strange to our Northern ways, and bring back to others pleasant blinks from* LANG SYNE, *they will have fully answered their purpose :*

> "*I softly trill my sparrow reed,*
>   *Blest if but one should like the twitter,*
> *Humbly I lay it down to heed,*
>   *A music or a minstrel fitter.*"

WILLIAM CARNIE.

Aberdeen, Christmas, 1890.

CONTENTS.

viii.   CONTENTS.

WAIFS OF RHYME.

WAIFS of a wilful fancy ; fruit of varied years :
Gladsome with fond memories ; chastened by sad tears.

WAIFS with little reason, perchance of doubtful rhyme ;
Spurrings of good comradeship to hasten tardy time.

WAIFS of changeful humour,—of bright and cloudy hours,
Treasured love and sorrow,—mingled thorns and flowers.

WAIFS scarce worth the storing.   Friend, take them as they stand.
They may recall, in days to come, a humble "vanish'd hand."

BONNIE DEESIDE.

When the birk tree like silver is shining,
   And the broom on the brae gleams like gold:
When the stag for the deep pool is pining,
   And the shorn ewe seeks shelter nor fold:
O ! then would I roam o'er the heather,
   Where often I've wandered in pride,
And twined fern and blue-bell together—
   Sae blithesome on bonnie Deeside.

I can see the grey auld Kirk o' Crathie—
   Balmoral and lythe Carnaquheen !
In the glen glints the hill-shepherd's bothie,
   Wi' dark Lochnagar far abeen.
I know not the journey before me !
   I care not what troubles betide !
While memory thus can restore me
   The joys o' lang-syne on Deeside.

The gloamin' brings back days departed,
   I see weel-kent faces ance mair ;
They come, the beloved and leal-hearted,
   From silence to solace my care.
Oh ! stay happy dreams of life's morning,
   Ye visions of past hours abide,
For ever ye bring in returning
   New blessings frae bonnie Deeside.

DAY DREAMING.

O ! that you and I were nutting
    In some pleasant English glade,
Our shelter from the summer's sun
    The hazel tree's dim shade,
With the woodlark and the linnet gay singing overhead.

Even now my fancy pictures
    The spot I long to see,
The home of thy blithe early days
    Ere first I looked on thee
And your sweet voice woke up feelings I deemed were dead in me.

I can trace the path thy footsteps
    Made glad with childish mirth ;
(To me there seems no holier place
    On this fair bounteous earth
Than the valley of thy girlhood—the cottage of thy birth).

Then I think that we are straying
    Silent 'mid that happy scene,
And there comes a peal of bridal bells
    From yon old church by the green,
And I muse, had we but earlier met, of what there *might* have been.

    .   .   .   .   .   .

'Twas a web of fancy's weaving—
    Stray, olden, golden gleams
Of youth's warm spring deceiving ;
    Hope's sun now colder beams,
And my love-thoughts, and my longings, are but vain and idle
    dreams.

ADDRESS

SPOKEN BY MRS. POLLOCK, ON BENEFIT NIGHT, IN

OLD HOUSE, MARISCHAL STREET.

[SCENE.—*An Apartment with table, sofa, &c. Casket on table, and books lying around. Mrs. Pollock sitting reading. After a pause she speaks.*]

Ah! well-a-day! 'tis utterly in vain,
I've scanned these volumes o'er and o'er again,
In hope to find some simple hint or cue
Might aid me in returning thanks [*advances to audience*] to you.
But no, 'tis fruitless all, "Love's Labour's Lost,"
And language fails me when I need it most.
True, I have found much measured phrase; but cold,
And foreign to the heart that would unfold
In words, brief, pointed, easily understood,
How much it feels of deepest gratitude
To those now round me who for years on years,
Have felt my gladness, ay! and shared my tears.
But this, you'll say, is scarce the time for weeping,
And Mrs. P. is used to public speaking:
Ay! true again; but feelings, fancies twine,
And memories crowd amain from Auld Langsyne.
⠀⠀⠀But let that pass. My friends, it seems an age
Since first I trod this dear familiar stage—
Since first, when tended by a father's hand,
I formed the youngest of a once famed band;
Since first, when but a girl, I strove to gain
Your approbation—and strove *not* in vain.

Since first I fell in love—I may reveal it—
With you, and you, and you [*points round theatre*]; why now
    conceal it?
Ah, me! how many scenes these words renew,
Since first I sought your—"hands," and found you true.
Then I got lots of vows, love gifts, and letters,
From youths who raved 'bout Cupid's wings and fetters.
Some of these *billet-doux* lie by me yet,
And one there is I never could forget.
        [*Goes to casket on table and takes out an old letter.*
It was so greenly soft, so full of Hymen's fire—
The writer was a bard, and thus he struck his lyre:—
        [*Reads from letter*]
    "Grant me, Apollo, all thy power,
      That I may fitly praise her;
    Fortune, I ask no other dower,
      Than just the charming Fraser."
Isn't that very innocent and pretty?
But mark the next verse of the fond youth's ditty,—
  [*Reads*]—"Her form it is divinely fair,"
That line, I'll vow, he must have stolen somewhere!
  [*Reads*]—"Her form it is divinely fair,
      Her eyes sharp as a ra*zer;*
    They've cut into my inmost heart,
      And there reigns sweet Miss Fraser."
Ay! once I "reign'd," you see, and had my day,
But those fond times are past—I've lost my sway,
For all love notes are now addressed expressly
To Langley, Jackman, or—Miss Clara Leslie.
Yet, why complain? Although these things are o'er,
Some joys I have will last for evermore,
Fond cherish'd thoughts—that while in time I grew
From Girl to Wife, ye aye were kind and true.

Whate'er my fate—where-'er my steps might roam,
Here still I found a welcome and a home.   [*Goes to casket.*
Within this casket treasured tokens lie
That link us all in one strong mutual tie ;
Symbols of seasons fled still prized and dear—
Some tempt a smile, while others claim a tear.
Rare hoarded things I would be loath to miss,
Records of days departed, such as this—
                    [*Displays large bill inscribed*
                              "BENEFIT OF MRS. RYDER."
Of later years I do not need to tell,
The parts I've played ye know them all full well.
I've had my share of sorrow and of gladness—
Our brightest hours have all a tinge of sadness—
I bow submissive—hold the proverb true—
"Ilk blade o' grass keps its ain drap o' dew."
                              [*Prompter's bell rings.*
But, hark ! I'm called, the Prompter's bell has rung,—
(When loosed, stop if you can a woman's tongue) !
Just let me say—and proudly too, with reason—
We're winding up " a most successful season."
No doubt we had our jars and opposition,
Yet there's no cause to mourn "a sad condition."
We've had to face of small guns quite a storm—
"Grand" Musical displays—"Great" Do-Re-Mi reform.
The College Question, too—with prosy Lectures
From Parsons, Doctors, Editors, and Rectors—
Parochial Cab-hires—Railway competition—
Mackenzie's Act—and Wombwell's "*Hexibition.*"
Poses Plastiques—bewitching raree-shows,
And other ways in which the money goes.
Yet, spite of all these matters to contend with,
I have a very pleasing tale to end with :

Ye have been kind—therefore let me be frank,
The Funds are up—we stand well at the bank !
    And now I'm done—yet ere I quit the scene,
One word at parting of our friend M'Lein.
He's gained *your* favour and approving smiles,
He's earned *my* gratitude and shared my toils,
Breathed words of comfort—wrought with willing hand—
Divined *my* wishes—*your* enjoyment planned.
From saddest woe *some* soothing balm is won—
I lost a Husband, but I found a Son.
    And now, kind friends—once more a brief farewell,
                    [*Prompter's bell rings sharply.*
Time's up—for hark ! the final warning bell.
May-day is here, and we must haste away
To other spheres our mimic parts to play.
Blithe Summer and fair Peace have come together,
The sword is sheathed, the swallow's winging hither.
When "wintr'y winds" drive Autumn from the plain
Here will we pitch our tent and sport again,
With new-culled sweets we'll speed to pleasure you :
Till then we part.   Adieu ! [*to Boxes.*] Adieu ! [*to Pit.*] Adieu !
    [*to Gallery.*]

REMEMBRANCE.

"Though parted, I shall never forget the days when I felt you had the power
to make me do anything."

I.

Were I a perfect Artist, with skill of brain and hand,
  I would set that simple legend in scroll of purest gold ;
With pearls from the utmost depths and gems from furthest strand,
  And its splendour should endazzle with a brilliancy untold:
        So beautiful and rare,
        So exquisite and fair,
  And its sheen would never darken nor its loveliness grow old.

II.

Had I the Poet's genius, the Singer's sacred fire,
  I would set that simple legend in verse to never die ;
The music should take birth as from some old prophetic lyre,
  And the Poet and the Singer in richest strain should vie—
        Now softly sweet, now loudly grand,
        Even as from full seraphic band :
  And the hymning chords should echo like the harmonies on high.

III.

Though no Artist skill be mine, nor gifted Minstrel power,
  I have set that simple legend on a life-enduring page :
Within my ever faithful breast 'tis treasured as a dower,
  To be erased nor altered by tempest nor by age :
        To last and ever linger
        Till Time's defacing finger
  Breaks the memory of a hopeless love, a lone heart's heritage.

TAM TEUCHIT'S REFLECTIONS AMANG
THE STOOKS.

I winder gin the hairst Meen shines wi' sic a glarin' licht
  On ither toons and pairishes as she glower'd doon here yestreen?
I'm sure a' owre the steadin' 'twas far mair day than nicht—
  I kenna hoo aboot this time they aye sen' sic a Meen !
Some o' oor chaps were greezin' beets, twa-three were readin' books,
And a' my airt I couldna get Jinse furth amang the stooks.

I like the Simmer weel eneuch, and I like the Winter tee ;
  The ane brings leefy hidin' holes—the tither's dark as pitch,
Sae that a tryste ye safe may haud and nae gleg body see,
  But losh me when the hairst begins ye scarce can heeze or hitch ;
The Meen lichts up a' corners, steals roon the dykes and neuks,
And sit fat side ye like ye're seen if oot amang the stooks.

On Feersday last the maister raise I saw 'tween four and five,
  Sae thinkin' he wad weir-awa gey early till his bed,
I tell't Jinse that we had a chance, if she wid but contrive
  To slip oot, when her wark was deen, ahint the auld neep shed—
We'd jink the lave, and baffle them, for a' their wiles and crooks
To catch us, and we'd hae an 'oor oorsels amang the stooks.

Jinse cam': O ! she wiz bonnie : if ye'd only seen her hair
  A' glancin' dark and wavy, wi' a ribbony roon her neck ;
I think that I could look at her until my een grew sair,
  Espeeshly whan she's on yon goon—a white-like tartan check ;
They brag aboot braw ladies in their dresses tuck'd wi' hooks,
They're better in fine drawin'-rooms than oot amang the stooks.

Weel, as I said, Jinse cam', and we sat kindly doon thegither,
  And happy were we there oor lanes, tho' I didna' like the Meen:
We spoke aboot the klyack nicht, then neist aboot the weather,
  And syne a sid stack in my teeth, and I wid steal a preen,
Sae I wiz slippin' roon my airm, whan baith oor wits forsook's
For wha appears but auld Sauchtoon gaun danderin' 'mang his stooks!

'We'll leid the morn, we'll leid the morn' (he mutters to himsel),
  'For tho' the corn's a thochty weet, 'twill mak' the meal the free-er.
Peer Jinse, her wee bit heart I fand wiz beatin' like a bell,
  She kent it wid be flittin' term if he should chance to see'er.
When jist in time, the cunnin' Meen behint a black clood jouks,
And in a jiffy we were aff, safe oot amang the stooks!

I said afore I liket weel the Winter and the Simmer,
  And I winna' say a wird against the Owtum or the Spring;
But I'm dootfu' o' a glarin' Meen, she mines me on some limmer
  That seeks to spy oot fairlies and syne clype ilka thing:
Yet hairstin, whan the crap is gweed, wirk ye wi' scythes or heuks,
Has mony joys and neen mair dear than coortin' 'mang the stooks.

———

SUMMER TIME.

(Part Song Words).

Soft falling showers refresh the flowers,
  The lark aloft is singing;
While blithe and free across the lea
  The school-boy's laugh is ringing,
The kine are browsing on the wold,
  The rose the morn perfumeth,
The violet sweet and marigold
  In mead and garden bloometh.

THE TIFF.

Ye manna grip me roun' the waist,
  Ye needna dawt my broo ;
Nor sall ye press yer cheek to mine,
  And syne slip to my moo :
I maybe like it weel eneuch—
  But ye deet to Crissy Dollar,
Sae Sandy lat me be—besides
  Ye're brackin a' my collar !

Ye needna speer what's ailin' me—
  Ye ken fine what I mean ;
Be quate—I winna lat ye noo !
  Fa wiz ye wi' yestreen ?
O, I ken a' aboot it lad—
  Sandy it's a shame
To tak' up wi' sae mony mair—
  There, now ! ye've split my kame.

Weel, if yer tellin' true and say
  Ye dinna care for Crissy—
I'll no be angry ony mair,
  And ye may tak' ae' kissie :
On Sunday nicht I'll meet ye tee—
  Tho' my feelin's ye've been hurtin,
And weer the bonnet that ye like—
  But ye mauna crush its curtain.

TO ANE FAR AWA'.

I'll sing a sang to thee, Tom,
    Though far frae me and hame ;
For leal thochts come o' thee, Tom,
    At the whisper o' thy name.
The waves may beat, the winds may blaw,
The Simmer bloom and Winter snaw,
But morn or nicht sall brak nor fa'
    That yer' nae dear to me, Tom.

'Tis years, O ! langsome years, Tom,
    Since last I saw yer' face ;
And sometimes I hae fears, Tom,
    Anither fills my place.
But hap what will, or come what may,
I'll ne'er forget or blame the day
I promised to be thine for aye,
    For thine I hope to be, Tom.

Ye'll read this simple sang, Tom,
    In yer hame across the sea ;
And ye'll ken I'm thinking lang, Tom,
    To look again on thee :—
To hear yer kindly voice ance mair,
To hear ye praise my face and hair,
To hear ye say that nane shall share
    Yer heart and hame, but me, Tom.

ADDRESS

BY MRS. POLLOCK, ON OPENING NIGHT OF SEASON,

MARISCHAL STREET THEATRE.

[SCENE—*A Parlour. Mrs. Pollock enters at stage door, and advancing to the middle of the stage, looks cautiously off at the wings.*]

They're busy there [*points behind scenes*], so I've stolen out a
    minute,
To try a speech—if I could but begin it ;
I fain would say how much I thank you all,
For thus responding to our early call,
O ! pleasant 'tis to look around and see
So many faces brimming o'er with glee ;
The Pit quite crammed—the Boxes, they will do,
And of the Gods—Gods ! what a jolly crew !
Some come to laugh at little Elliot's frolic,
And not a few to welcome—Mrs. Pollock.
For many griefs your presence makes amends—
Who could be dumpish with such "troops of friends !"
Friends, young and old—wedged everywhere so tight,
And all to grace us on our Opening Night :
Thanks, patrons, thanks—each kindly heart and face—
O, "may your shadows never *here* be less."
    Dear, generous friends, but four short months are past,
Since in a scene like this we parted last,
I promised then, from "fields and pastures new,"
To cull fresh sweets to tempt and pleasure you,

So I have roamed like some blithe busy bee
(Forgive the self-complacent similie),
And, stored, brought home a goodly "swarm" with me;
At least *I* think so—you will justly try,
And let us know the verdict by-and-by.   ˙
I hope they'll stand the test—and so may thrive,
And bring much honey to our little hive.
Old Time proves all things—he will prove this too—
Meanwhile, pray tell me, will the Theatre do?—

> ˉ [*Points round Theatre.*

The Queen Bee roved, but when across the Border,
She left not *drones* to put the house in order !
      If I can read aright those nods and smiles,
Your taste approves the artist's careful toils.
Our labour thus has not been spent in vain,
So now a word about our year's campaign.
We purpose, then, if Fortune plays us fair,
To bring forth novelties both "rich and rare "—
Love Dramas—where some interesting maiden
Is woo'd—forsaken—then with anguish laden,
In tears, and sighing sore with hapless moan,
Wins you to make her sorrow half your own.
Then changed the theme, we'll paint in martial story,
How Britons climbed steep "Alma's hill to glory ! "
And when chill Christmas comes, by trick and rhyme,
We'll frighten Care with merry pantomime,
Yet ever keeping open ears and eyes,
For rising "stars," in home and foreign skies.
All this we'll do, and more, if *ye* prove heedful,
And keep the wheels agoing with the—needful !
Trusting our mimic efforts ne'er may fail
"To point a moral, or adorn a tale."

But while devising new, be not afraid
The grand old drama's power shall ever fade.
Shakespere—but second since the world began
To fathom Nature, or to measure Man—
Shakespere, immortal ! thy life-glowing page
Shall still shed lustre on the modern stage !
Even now, methinks, thy chief creations rise,
And tread these boards in old familiar guise.
See ! who approaches—'tis the fiendish Jew—
" The pound of flesh—I here demand my due ;
I stand for judgment."   [*Gives imitations.*
                              Soft, we have a change,
The sweetest love tale in the drama's range—
'Tis Romeo to fair Juliet fond plaint makes,
As angel " light through yonder window breaks."——
" It is my lady, O ! it is my love,
O, that she knew she were !
She speaks, yet she says nothing.   What of that ?
Her eye discourses, I will answer it.
I am too bold ; 'tis not to me she speaks :
Two of the fairest stars in all the heaven,
Having some business, do entreat her eyes
To twinkle in their spheres till they return.
What if her eyes were there, they in her head ?
The brightness of her cheek would shame those stars,
As daylight doth a lamp ; her eyes in heaven
Would through the airy region stream so bright
That birds would sing and think it were not night."——
      But hark ! who calls with such impetuous force :—
"A horse, a horse, my kingdom for a horse ;
I think there be six Richmonds in the field,
Five have I slain to-day."
                    The bell hath pealed,

And hush ! the Thane's wife dreaming comes this way.
She speaks—"Out damnéd spot ! out, out, I say,   .   .
Fie, my Lord, fie ! a soldier and afeard ?   .   .   .   .
Come, come, come, come, to bed, to bed, to bed."——
    Scarce hath she left when, lo ! the clang of swords
Rings from the plain with loud and angry words ;
Macbeth's at bay—he fights—"Lay on Macduff,
And damned be he that first cries hold, enough."

    But I presume *you've* quite enough of this—
Though, really, you must own, 'twas not amiss.
Yet if 'twere wanted I might change the scene,
And give a touch of—Melnotte and Pauline ;
Or coming nearer home, with Highland fire and vigour,
Mount plaid and plume, and shout, "my name's Macgregor."

    But all this by-and-by—'t is getting late,
The Prompter beckons [*looks out*]—will not longer wait.
On things in general, I need scarcely touch,
There's nothing stirring, or, at most, not much ;
There are no mighty questions to propound—
The Links are—*quiet*, and—the Czar is crown'd.
Just one word more—Walk from the city forth,
A bounteous harvest decks the kindly earth ;
The ruddy reaper sweating o'er his scythe,
With steady stroke keeps all the field full blithe ;
The farmer smiles to see the laden wain
Hie cheerily homewards with the golden grain.
Now, look within—*our* harvest has begun—
Shall *we* smile proudly when the season's done ?
Shall we reap richly—have a fair reward
For studious midnights, and for labour hard ?
That lies with you, and there I let it lie,
Hoping the best, and with that hope—Good-bye !

"OUR" PURVEYOR-ROYAL.

I ken a winsome wifikie that keeps a snug bit shoppie,
(It's nae ane o' the temptin' kind whaur ye may get a "droppie,")
For ever brisk and business-like wi' mony gweed things packit
If hungry Frenchmen e'er come here they will be sure to sack it.
Gin ye wad learn its whaur-aboots gang up the Windmillbrae—
But the number or the corner I mauna print or say,
For that wad be ower personal, and I might for my folly
Lose baith the service and respect o' blithesome Jeannie Jolly.

O, Jeannie's skill is dear to me, and will be evermair—
And lang, I pray, that Jeannie's life auld ruthless Time may spare ;
For whaur's a cook o' Jeannie's worth—sae tidy and sae keen
As sharp and bright, frae morn till night, as ony new made preen ?
If ye gaze into her window and yer moo it disna water,
Your thrapple maun be gizzand, like a chiel's fresh aff the batter ;
The bairns stan' roun't in boorichies, and whisper aft "O, golly,
I wiss I bide-it aye in there wi' happy Jeannie Jolly.

Feich ! fa wid live on blubber stuff, and cauld ice made to jelly ?
I pity folk that *maun* tak' things enough to freeze their belly—
Their salads vile o' eggs and ile mixed up in sic a mess,
I canna think hoo Christian men daur ower them say a grace !
Tairts, turtle soops, and sic like trash to me were ne'er a treat,
Nor yon green gear a frien' o' mine ca's "just kye's common meat."
To see hoo fashion hardens folk it's really melancholy—
Ye'll get nae sic unnateral stews fae kindly Jeannie Jolly.

c

Jist study Jeannie's stock-in-trade : Look at the pottit-heid
Set oot in canty bowlies there : examine next her breid ;
Observe the fresh-pluck'd chuckies syne, hoo temptingly they
    hing,
Wi' "dainty dishes in a row micht sit afore a king ; "
Her puddins they are peerless, and speakin' o' her tripe,
O' mortal bliss supreme and full it is the test and type !
My brakfast I wad gladly mak' oot o' a mornin' rollie,
If I were sure o' tripe at nicht prepared by Jeannie Jolly.

Nae wonder Jeannie's popular, sma' marvel she's respeckit—
The best o' Ladies in the toon, in silks and satins deckit,
Ca' aft at her bit shoppikie, weel kennan they'll get there
The fattest, tenderest goose or hen on whilk their Lords may fare ;
They ken that Jeannie's honour bright, that a' *she* sells is clean,
Nae dirt e'er grows 'neath her thoom nails, nor roost on knife or
    speen.
If ye're to hae a pairty send roun' yer servant Polly
To say yer wantin' " something nice "—then trust to Jeannie Jolly.

.   .   .   .

Last night there was a Regal feast—and who was King but he
That writes this idle rhyme : The guests—his wife and children
    three.
No lacquered valets hung around, no pert inquiring page—
This Sovereign pair do "serve themselves till their bairns shall
    come of age."
Before the Noble household lay five " white puds " in a plate,
One dish of tripe, a jug of milk—and there they supped in state,
Yet ere the meal was ended quite, they gave one loyal volley
To their own Purveyor-Royal—the matchless Jeannie Jolly.

A FACTORY LASSIE'S SANG.

(Air: The Kye comes hame).

My lad he is a bonnie lad, and bides in Aberdeen,
He's aye richt frank and kindly, sae pintit aye and clean,
An' tho' I'm but a lassie yet and wirkin at the mill,
He's liket me since first we met, and says he likes me still,—
   He says he likes me still, he says he likes me still,
   Sae I'll try to be as gweed's I can, tho' wirkin at the mill.

I ken some folk look doon on us and ca' us orra trag,
But hearts may love and thochts be pure tho' cover'd by a rag ;
On Feersday nicht when wages comes I pay a' that I'm due,
An' weir the auld claes oot until I'm able to get new,—
   Until I can get new, takin' up nae shooster's bill,
   For I'll try to be aye clear o' debt tho' wirkin at the mill.

There's mony lassies that we meet wad like to win my lad,
And whan they see me gaun wi' him its like to pit them mad ;
They think I'm far aneath them, an' wid treat me wi' disdain,
But I never wore a bonnet yet that wisna' a' my ain,—
   That wisna' a' my ain, sae lat them jeer wha will,
   Ane needna haud their heid aye doon tho' wirkin at the mill.

There's Peggy she's a polisher, Jean's at the envelopes,
Flo and Kate wad fain be ladies, an' sae they serve in shops ;
Jemima stitches printet books, Miss Alice shoos at hame,
Sly Annie cures provisions, and there's some I wadna name,—
   There's some I wadna name, bit wi' a' their airt and skill,
   They canna ding the lassie oot that's wirkin' at the mill.

My lad he's nae a baker, they hae to rise owre seen,
Nor yet is he a sailor, for fa' wid lie their leen ;
The sooter nor the tailor chaps on Monday's winna wirk,
An' I never kent a kamemacker that gaed to ony kirk,—
  They never fyle the kirk bit play mischief and ill,
  Yet some o' them hae made gweed men to lassies at the mill.

My dear lad's name ye'd like tae ken, bit that I mauna tell,
For love is nae the richt heart love that clashes o' itsel ;
He's maybe doon the Fittie way, or oot at Ferryhill,
Or maybe he's nae far fae me an' wirkin at the mill,—
  He's maybe at the mill, maybe Tom or Jim or Bill,
  An' he's promised in a year or twa to tak' me fae the mill.

TO ———

O, Marion, my Marion,
    The rose is on thy cheek ;
Yet Marion, fair Marion,
    Ye tremble while I speak :
I look into your eyes and see
A love-licht glancin' back to me,
And then sic thochts I hae o' thee,
    I daurna tell them Marion.

My Marion, my Marion,
    I canna read your smiles ;
Nor Marion, sweet Marion,
    Can I resist your wiles,—
For O ! sae saft's this heart o' mine,
I'm sometimes like my wits to tyne
When gazing on sic charms as thine,
    Then spare me, spare me, Marion.

ADDRESS.

SPOKEN AT THE NETHERLEY AND PORTLETHEN
VOLUNTEER ASSEMBLY, 1861.

In days gone by within our rugged land
Rude tumult raged, by jealous faction fanned ;
Clan fought with clan—the wild deer from his corrie,
Flew not more swift than brethren sought the foray ;
Kindred forgot its ties ; Love knew nor grace nor art
To soothe the vengeful nature of the Gael heart.

A happier era dawned. Peace with her heavenly smile
Benignant came to bless our dear loved Scottish isle.
No more from castled steep and rampart high
Proud challenge waved or rang the battle cry ;
No beacon lights blazed up : the hill-tops dimmed their fires,
Nor longer signals sped, as speed the worded wires.
Peace rose and reigned ; men "hostile feuds," forbore—
" To ploughshares beat their swords, and studied war no more."

Thus rested our old land ; Art, Science, Letters, grew
Far mightier in their strength than steel or shaft of yew.

But change must have its sway. Across the channel came
A vaunting threat that stirred the ancient flame.
A seeming friend—an ally for occasion
Muttered a tone whose echoing breathed "invasion."
That tone must have reply ; and soon the whispered hum
Of careless doubt re-echoed—" Let him come :
Ay let him ! and though peace hath wrought her charms
We have not quite forgot our former skill in arms."

Wide rolled the summons.   Heart with heart then beat
In unison of purpose.   Village and crowded street,
Sequestered valley, farm-field, and quiet glen
Saw hurried mustering of undaunted men—
Men loving freedom which their fathers won,
Resolved the sire should still live in the son.
The summons rolled and at the call appears
A hundred thousand patriot Volunteers !

A humble unit of that glorious band,
Thus firmly knit to guard their native land—
We—Portlethen's sons, the men of Netherley—
To our loved country willing service pay.
Though few our numbers, yet amid that host
Have we not some good right to count and boast ?
Who gave to England her first Champion Shot ?
Who for old Scotland's fame so nobly fought ?
Who from all compeers bore the bell away ?—
Who but young Edward of fair Netherley.
We taught the world this task—"Devotion honour earns,"
"As the auld cock craws, be sure the young ane learns."

Our Captain, too, our chiefest boast and pride
Whose deeds have rung 'yond Europe's empire wide ;
Where is the arm that may with his compare
'Gainst mountain hart or bird that soars in air ?
No braggart he, or idle dreaming talker,
Let acts approve the man—"The Old Deer-Stalker."

Honour where honour's due : so lads again I say
Busk ye your bonnets braw—Portlethen—Netherley !

VERSES

"Sir David Lindsay of the Mount, Lord Lyon King-at-Arms,
Still is thy name of high account, and still thy verse hath charms;"
And while the world hath ear for song or deeds of chivalry,
The Lindsay's fame, the Lindsay's claim, shall ne'er forgotten be—
    True gallant Scottish Gentlemen for all—for every time.

Unfold the records of the past, old Scotland's peerless roll—
Count ye the Warriors, Statesmen, Poets, emblazoning the scroll ;
And say 'mid all the names that stir the pulses of the heart,
If Lindsay's race for valour, grace, doth not play noblest part ?
    True gallant Scottish Gentlemen for all—for every time.

Ah! "Scotsmen ken that gallant men" the Lindsay line hath been,
From Otterburn to Alma's height have flashed their weapons keen ;
"The Stars our Camp, God our Defence," bore crested squire and
    knight—
To Scotland's weal aye fest and leal—then Heaven defend the right !
    True doughty Scottish Gentlemen for all—for every time.

And still the Lindsay verse has charms to wile the hours away,
And never will its Music cease while lives *Auld Robin Gray ;*
For men will list and maidens weep in cot and courtly hall,
O'er Jeannie's faith and Jamie's wraith, for " Love is Lord of all"—
    In camp and grove, fond Love—fause Love—ruler of every time.

And Love should be my theme to-night, could I strike fitting chord,
For golden rings and silken strings outshine now shield and sword :
A comely "Lass of Lancashire," with guileless grace and spell,
Hath witched away our Master gay in Love's domain to dwell—
  And spend the hours in bridal bowers : God speed the merry time.

"The glory of the Children are their Fathers"—hath been writ—
And the Lindsays, Wilbrahams, Stanleys, to-day in clanship knit,
With noble heritage of fame, renown, and acres wide—
To ward and keep, to sow and reap, dower our young groom and
    bride—
  Well tochered they to climb life's brae and meet the coming time.

The summer sun shines brightly o'er Dunecht's fair woods and
    towers ;
O come sweet "Rose o' Lindsaye," bloom 'mang our buds and
    flowers :
Come with your lightsome English smile to cheer our Northern
    hame—
And ear' or late The Master's Mate shall find us aye the same—
  True-hearted Scottish Gentlemen, sons of the olden time.

THE PLOUGH.

My song shall be of the noblest art
    That man hath ever known ;
Whose labours glad hearth, home, and heart—
    The cottage and the throne.
For they who raise our daily bread
    Deserve our thanks I vow ;
So hurrah, hurrah, for the scythe and spade,
    The Farmer and his Plough.
            Then brothers all in hut and hall,
            In chorus join me now ;
            And pray success may ever bless
            The work of the goodly Plough.

Let others sing of the sword and shield,
    Of blood and the battle plain ;
I have no wish such arms to wield,
    They neither bring good nor gain.
But with nobler brand I'd take my stand,
    And corn not men I'd mow,
For 'twere better far if the weapons of war,
    Were turned to the Scythe and Plough.
            Then the blade I'd bear is a good ploughshare,
            A trusty one I trow ;
            My crest a hive with a spade and scythe,
            My motto—SPEED THE PLOUGH.

We will toast the Queen, and our native land,
  The Pen and the mighty Press ;
The Wire and Steam that at man's command,
  Have conquered time and space.
But while we sit round the festive hearth,
  And honour to all allow,
We will *use* not *abuse* the fruits of the earth
  For they all spring up from the Plough.
    Then hurrah for the arms that till the farms,
    Who harrow, reap, and sow,
    To the flail, the flake, the hoe and rake,
    And ever GOD SPEED THE PLOUGH.

MADRIGAL.

Sadly in a vale alone,
    Sat the fair nymph Vilapone,—
Sighing, crying, desolate—
Longing for her forest mate.

Hush ! a voice sounds thro' the grove,—
"Vilapone, where art thou, love ! "
    No longer sighing,
        But quick replying,—
Meeting—greeting.

Soon the woods melodious ring :
List the lay the fond twain sing,—
    "With thou not near,
      Life's sand seems run,—
    When thou art here,
      Love pales the sun."

"THERE'S AYE SOME WATER WHAUR
THE STIRKIE DROONS!"

My auld Grannie had a fret, O weel I mind it yet,
 For aften roun' my memory and in my lug it croons ;
Whan curious things cam' oot, she wid shak' her heid in doot,
 Wi', "There's aye some water, laddie, whaur the stirkie droons!"

There wiz henpeck'd Lawyer Rae, the Laird o' Scutterbrae,
 His wife, wi' dress and denner-gien, ootran a' common bouns ;
The Laird's gear grew fu' sma', and whan he dwyned awa'—
 Folk said—"There's aye some water whaur the stirkie droons!"

Mrs. Councillor McFell—sae at least weel-wishers tell—
 Is subject maist untimeously to sudden faints and swoons—
But the virtue o' a dram, quickly dissipates her dwam ;
 Ay ! there's medicine in *some* waters tho' the stirkie droons !

Ye ken cripple Tailor Black—he's a wylin tongue and slack—
 And ye min' the bonnie servin' lassie up at Lucky Broon's !
They've been sessioned baith thegither—but ye mauna heed folks'
  blether,
 Tho' there be some water ever whaur the stirkie droons!

Sly hoastin' Heckler Fyfe wish'd to insure his life,
 But whan he wiz examin'd there were heard sepulchral soun's :
His life it wizna "gweed," for the doctor wrote this screed—
 "*Aqua pura quantum suff:*" and the stirkie droons !

There's blithesome Charlie Senter oor Parish kirk precenter,
  Grows nervous aft on Sundays pitchin' up his psalms and tunes ;
The lad's a staunch tee-totaller, but bein' by trade a bottler,
  He mistak's the strength o' water—and the stirkie droons !

I've a frien'—he's maybe here—whaun he waukens and feels queer—
  Try's to look as sage as Wisdom—while his heid wi' Folly stouns ;
But suggest that he's been fou', and he'll swear it isna true—
  Yet we ken there's aye some water whaur the stirkie droons !

Oor wee Jock bides oot at nicht, till his mither's in a fricht—
  Syne threeps he wiz " deein' naething, wi' a lot o' ither loons ; "
But if ye his pouches rype, ye'll fin something like a pipe—
  And a smell betok'nin water whaur the stirkie droons !

Mrs. Gab, she gied a pairty, and ye min' we a' were hearty,
  Yet she vows she's never seen sin'-syne twa o' her silver spoons,
While the last to tak' their tea was either you or me—
  And she hints, " There *maun* be water whaur the stirkie droons!"

Gin yer cairt-wheel should tak' fire, mair grease is its desire,
  It hiz grow'n dry as rosit in its mony weary rouns ;
Sae I maun stop my verse, for ye hear I'm turnin' hearse—
  Yer health : " There's aye some water whaur the stirkie droons!

EPILOGUE

SPOKEN BY MRS. POLLOCK, AT CLOSE OF SEASON,

ABERDEEN THEATRE ROYAL.

So, once again the parting hour has come,
And, like the schoolboy loath to leave his home
When holiday is o'er, we sadly pack our kit,
Bid loving friends adieu, and, heart-sore, haste to quit.
Yet, like the lad who hies to book and task,
Of coming joys in Hope's bright sun we bask ;
Far in the future with fond eyes we strain
And dream of days when we'll be "back again."
Be timely back—to weep, laugh, dance, and sing,
And hear your gladsome shout—"the play's the thing."
Be back—to strut kings, beggars, wits, and fools,
As earnest, ay! as—laddies at the bools.
Still, ere we go, a word or two I'd say—
Indeed, I'd *scold* you if I had my way :
For surely you must own 'tis most ungallant,
Alike of lady, gentleman, and callant,
That you of late have not been oftener near us
With glistening eye, and ready hand to cheer us,
When well you know our open door solicits
Your ever welcome step and frequent visits.
'Tis shameful, cruel—my anger is so deep,
If it would have effect, I—I—I—really think I'd weep.
                 [*Comes forward to front and listens.*
  Pray, did you speak, Sir?—Please to say't again.
O ! yes ; you think me in a railing vein !

[*To the audience farthest off.*

My friend here says that this is something more
Than what he paid for at the Theatre door :
He'd have it stated duly in the bill
In taking type, with all the printer's skill,
That, " For the benefit of Mrs. P.,
Will be produced—A Woman Ta'en the Gee."
So *you* smile too, and my sad tale you mock it—
There's little laughter in an empty pocket.

[*Shakes dress, and a jingling is heard.*

No ; not *quite* empty ; a *something* still is over,
Will help to keep's in *grass* if not in *clover*.
The truth is this—and now I speak sincerely,
That after weighing matters fair and clearly,
The Season, on the whole, has paid itself,
So that we're not just yet laid on the shelf.
But let us own, we've had an uphill fight,
'Tween Circus, Waxwork, Concerts every night ;
While spare cash went for music Bells, and Hall,
Those Grand Assemblies, and that *sweet* Trades' Ball.
But each thing has its hour—why, therefore, fret ?
I'll hopeful bide " the good time coming yet."
    Meanwhile, I trust no fault you have to find
With my share of the work ?

                I thank you, now—*that*'s kind.
Week after week brought forth some shining " star,"
Whose bright attraction reached us from afar.
(Here I may state, in case my memory slips,
It was not I produced the late Eclipse.)
Week after week, you had the primest fare
Served up with taste, and all were asked to share ;
And if *all* did not come our feast to grace,
The cause, I dare say, is not hard to guess.

Dull trade, hard times, the money market tight,
Gave other things than Theatres a fright.
But now the worst is past, the panic's at an end,
And everything gives promise fast to mend ;
Bear witness ye who wanting room to sit,
Stand by me now—on this my Benefit.

But time and tide wait not for man or woman ;
I see my cue, the Prompter 'gins to summon.
So, then, good-bye : may a' that's guid attend ye—
May fortune ne'er look glum, but aye befriend ye.
Fair be the flowers ye pu' in nature's garden ;
Sweet be the maids ye woo—Ladies, I beg pardon :
All maids are sweet when woo'd ; 'tis only after
That—
                    You men, I scorn your laughter—
And so proceed to say, as said it must be,
The parting word—Farewell : I fondly trust we
Here may meet when some six months are run,
To teach you by our tears, and please you with our fun ;
To cheat old Winter of his dreary reign,
And make ye blithe to see us "back again."

"LIVE AND LET LIVE."

Live and let live be your watchword for ever,
  The bond of true union between man and man ;
A union that time nor contention shall sever,
  A link in the chain forming heaven's perfect plan.
Though the path the poor travel be careworn and lowly,
  And scanty their portion to store or to give—
Remember the mite of the widow was holy,
  And earth's noblest maxim is—Live and let live.

Live and let live—wherefore stand strangely parted,
  The best of us boast but a fast fleeting day ;
The richest of men is the man largest hearted,
  Whose hand can the dictates of duty obey.
When the green grass waves o'er us and friends tell our story,
  May this prove the brief, faithful record they give—
" He was neighbour to all, to do good was his glory,
  For the rule of his conscience was—Live and let live."

Live and let live—we have all our set places,
  And most of us fare quite as well as we ought ;
There are lessons of wisdom in cares and distresses,
  As the sweetest of pleasure by labour is bought.
Never fret though the sunshine of luck fall on others,
  There are heart joys the world cannot lessen or give—
Go on your way gaily, count all men as brothers,
  And mind the old maxim of—Live and let live.

TO CELIA.

Nay! not "too bold" my Celia fair;
    Press closer still those lips of thine,
More glowing sweet and warm, I swear,
    Than July rose or Cyprian wine.
Clasp that soft arm around my neck,
    Caress with tender touch my brow;
Come grief or joy—come fame or wreck—
    I ne'er was nearer heaven than now.

My Celia, whatsoe'er my fate—
    Whate'er the tale of after years,
Though sorrow should beside me wait,
    And hope accompanied be by tears;
While memory lasts and reason reigns
    I'll ne'er forget the hour divine,
When bound in Love's resistless chains
    I held thy yielding breast to mine.

Dear Celia, charmer, here to-night
    Thy presence haunts me like a spell;
I see a face all radiant, bright,
    I breathe a wish I may not tell;
In fancy I embrace thy form,
    A thousand kisses try to win;
I feel a touch brings calm or storm—
    "The touch that makes the whole world kin."

AGGIE'S NEW GOON.

(A Nursery Lilt.)

O ! Aggie has gotten a bonnie new goon,
O ! Aggie has gotten a bonnie new goon,
It's a wee winsome strippie wi' flounces a' roon—
And it fits her fu' finely her bonnie new goon.

Jist look at her waistie sae jimp and sae sma'—
There's nae ither lassie's can match it ava ;
Ilka time that I meet her my heart gies a stoon—
She's sae neat and complete in her bonnie new goon.

Wi' a facie as fair as the dawnin' o' morn,
Her cheekies as red as the rose on the thorn ;
An' lips, O ! to kiss them a saint micht boo doon,
Sae sweet is the lass wi' the bonnie new goon.

O gin I should win her an ca' her my ain,
Then Fate do your warst, I've a balm for ilk pain,
Wi' her in my bosom dark fortune may froon,
If bless'd wi' the lass in the bonnie new goon.

Then blithely I'll sing o' my Aggie's new goon,
Its winsome wee strippies an' flounces a' roon,
To me there's nane like it in country or toon—
She's the joy o' my heart wi' her bonnie new goon.

ADDRESS

SPOKEN BY MANAGER M^CNEILL, AT CLOSE OF SEASON,
ABERDEEN THEATRE ROYAL.

"Should auld acquaintance be forgot?"   These words
Touch like a spell the full heart's tenderest chords ;
Gone days come back that long had fled away,
And joys return we wish would ever stay.
Lost hours of Love and Friendship: who, oh! who hath not
Some hidden memories of the past that ne'er may be forgot?
The dear, old, simple, sweet refrain hath magic in its tone
To summon back our "life's young day," tho' years on years have
    flown.
      And as a spell these words to-night serve me,
For "auld acquaintance" is the witcherie
That weaves the magnet links that draw you here
.To say, good-bye, and give a parting cheer.
For, like a ship that hath discharged its stores
Hies boldly forth again for distant shores,
Fearless of racking wind or raging foam,
To gather wealth anew for those at home—
So we, our spoils unloaded, canvas all unfurled,
Prepare to shift the scene of our bright mimic world :
We haste to reap for you fresh intellectual sport,
And bring the harvest home to this loved little port.
      Yet, ere we fairly start upon our duteous trip,
'Tis meet I should recount my season's stewardship ;
Show you, as 'twere, the vessel's log-book.   Be it so ;
I'll gladly pay a debt I am most proud to owe.
Well, then, in sterling terms of pounds and pence—
(And terms I know none likelier to convince),

We're sounder at the Bank than e'er before we stood—
We carry a round sum forward, and our credit's good.
With gratitude, my friends, I cheerfully confess,
The season closing now has been a rare success.
Our tidy craft, by willing workers manned,
Has never, since I took the helm in hand,
Made voyage so pleasant, met more favouring gales,
Or found the tide of Fortune steadier with our sails.

     For this be honour given where honour's justly due,—
Therefore, my heartfelt thanks I humbly offer *you.*
Without your generous presence—ever welcome smiles—
Of small avail, indeed, were our best art or wiles.
And then, a meed of praise I tender to my crew—
Right faithful, ready shipmates all the season through.

     Who to name first I'm really at a loss.—
Eh! did I hear a whisper which meant the Misses Ross?
The hint is good.   Who now—"The fair girl with the blarney,"
You're right : You mean, of course, our Irish gem, Kate Kearney.
The sprightly Birkett, too, has title to a line—
So neat and light of foot as tricky Columbine.
And now, the sterner sex claim notice.   Let me see—
Who's worthiest in your judgment—Waverley?
I thought so.   Then Barrett, Coutts, Macfarren, Kay,
Wharton and Wilmot—but you deem that I
Have left two from the list.   Ah! much I'd be to blame
If I forgot the Watsons, each and both, to name.

     Nor, while we thus divide our wintry laurel-wreath,
Omit the stars—the Webbs, Talbot, and graceful Heath ;
And, young folks, be ye sure, for reasons good I don't
Neglect what's due to Pantomime—our Jones and Pont.
My own "guid wife" too, still my anxious labour shares—
Though kept behind the scenes by—yes growing family cares !

And say, while naming those who yield delight and frolic—
"Should auld acquaintance be forgot" and Mrs. Pollock?

And now, again with gratitude sincere,
I thank each friend—each brother Volunteer.
This little house, meanwhile so full and bright,
Will soon be lone and dull.   Gone the sweet light
Of cheerful beaming eyes.   Fled all those happy faces,
And nought but Fancy left to fill the vacant places.
Yet oft, as memory fondly from the vanish'd past recalls
Loved and familiar tones and haunts, so I within these walls
Shall often rest and wander wafted by the wizard spell
Of "auld langsyne" that brings you here to list, and say—FARE-
WELL!

PART SONG.

Ho! groom bring forth my gallant steed,
   To horse, and on with me;
We'll buckle gear, and gaily speed
   A captive maid to free.
And bid thy comrades arm for fight,
   And follow in our train;—
Love-laden we'll return to-night,
   Or come back not again.

When we have reached her father's gate,
   A bugle note thou'lt wind;
And if they bid us lingering wait,
   We'll point to those behind.
For love ne'er palls at strength of walls,
   Nor yields to parent scorn;—
The crest I wear—the name I bear
   May match with any born.

THE LAIRD O' MORKEU.

Awa wi' your Emperors, Sultans, Rajahs,
We care nae for Khedive, Porte, Pope, or Pachas ;
To nane sic we're subject—the monarch we loe
He reigns and gies law frae the tap o' Morkeu.

The Laird o' Morkeu sits afar on a hicht,
His candle ye'll see't in the sma' oors o' nicht,
Nae bushel for him—save a bushel to brew
Wi' licht aye confeerin' aroon blithe Morkeu.

He's canny and carefu', stan's up for his ain,
Yet Poverty ne'er sought his ha' door in vain ;
There's nae a bit bird thing, lark, lintie, or doo,
But coonts on free aumrie to crumbs at Morkeu.

The Laird he lives single—owns nae household chips.
He likes weel the ladies, but doots wedlock grips ;
He jinks wi' fond widows, pits maids in a stew,
Then lats the heat cool, and roams free 'roon Morkeu.

He's soun on theology—firm in the faith,
Aye cosh wi' the clergy whatever their claith,
Sly Priest and slee Presbyter—auld kirk or new,
They a' hae a share in the creed o' Morkeu.

In the toon a keen trader o' credence and fame
The Laird hauds his head wi' the proodest ye'll name ;
'Mang lang rows o' figures, the learned Mackildhu
Maun aften sing sma' when confrontin' Morkeu.

He's fit for a Provost, or even a Deen—
Weel gifted wi' speech, he says ditto to neen ;
He'll nail you on politics, science, airt, oo'—
He's a wide range o' thocht, has the Laird o' Morkeu.

The flowers are unborn yet in garden or field,
That sweetness and joy to the Laird cannot yield ;
His coat button-hole glows a marvel in hue,
When summer is bloomin' 'roon bonny Morkeu.

Jist see him at glomin'—leal frien's by him set,
The lamp o' wit lichtet—cheer, plenty and het ;
Syne follows a rubber at short whist or loo,
And happiness hallows the house o' Morkeu.

Ye ken the Laird's kith—there's the said learned Mac,
At kirkstile or coonter, keen aye for a crack ;
The thread o' a sermon, the hair o' a soo',
He'll split or explain wi' the best at Morkeu.

With courtly salute comes the Chief o' Sang-Schule,
His hand and heart open to love-darg or dool ;
For big nibbet words he'd blake Gentile or Jew—
It's whisper'd he sometimes dumfounders Morkeu.

And sib to the same sits a queer rhymster chiel,
Whiles wantin' in ballast, but scarcely a feel ;
When psalms or when sangs shape the crook o' his mou',
There's nae coontin' tumblers or time at Morkeu.

But thinkna' low voices ne'er chasten the glee,
When the wine micht grow red and the tongue wad gang free ;
Soft words, aye in season, like sweet fa'in dew,
Refreshen and gladden hame-life at Morkeu.

Then lang life we'll pray for oor Bachelor Laird,
Wha'ever is ta'en—he canna be spared ;—
Yet when the cord breaketh and Time claims his due,
May the Laird rest in peace—as he lived at Morkeu.

"COME."

Come, lady, and gladden my lone little home,
  Come, bid a waiting heart fondly rejoice ;
Come as sweet sunshine and music, love, come,
  With the light of thy presence, the sound of thy voice.

Though the morning of youth hath its place in the past,
  And the noontime of life fades to calm eventide,
Yet the gloaming were joyous if round it were cast
  The charm of contentment with thee by my side.

O come and be near me when shades of night fall,
  Come counsel and cheer when by friendship forgot ;
And mine be the tribute to bear with thee all
  The sorrows the Master may will in thy lot.

Forgive, when we meet, if my words are but few,—
  Forgive, if my lips leave their longing untold,
Believe the old proverb is potent and true,
  That speech is but silver while silence is gold.

Then come, lady, come, to my lone little home,
  Come, bid a waiting heart fondly rejoice ;
Bring sunshine for shadow around me, love, come,
  With the light of thy presence, the sound of thy voice.

VOLUNTEER PART SONG.

(*Air: The Hardy Norseman*).

Nay ! never say our arms are weak,
   Or that our hearts are cold ;
The blood still rusheth to the cheek
   At brave deeds done of old.
We softly tread where rest the dead—
   A true devoted band ;
We boast their name, we chant their fame,
   Who kept our father-land.

Nay ! never say though on the wall,
   The sword hangs in its sheath,
That silent now to honour's call
   We covet not its wreath :
We pray for peace with love's increase—
   But war's red flag unrolled—
The sword we'll clasp with ready grasp
   As in the days of old.

Nay ! never say our native shore
   Shall know the invader's sway ;
Our fathers stood her shield of yore—
   We claim that right to-day ;
From busy town, and breezy down,
   Shall gather on her strand,
Hearts warm and true, arms strong nor few—
   To guard the dear old land.

HOOTY-TOOTY.

Last night I talked thus with my bird,—
 Thou pretty warbler tell me, do,
Hast ever seen—hast ever heard,
 Lady like my mistress true,
Rare in mien, and rich in beauty?—
 Quoth the bird—" Twit, Hooty-Tooty ! "

I bade the bird approve my choice,
 For she was gentle as the dove ;
With gracious smile, sweet eyes, and voice
 Soft as ever whisper'd love :
Mine her heart and her's my duty,
 Still the bird chirp'd " Hooty-Tooty ! "

I warmly vowed my mistress young
 Was pure as new-born flower in spring ;
Had pleasant temper and a tongue—
 Here the bird began to sing,—
" Loving maids are precious booty,
 But they're women—Hooty-Tooty ! "

MILK AND SCONES.

Speak nae to me o' turtle soup,
    Wi' oysters fae the sea ;
To French snail pies I'll never stoop,
    Nor common puddock bree :
My thochts ging back to lythe Lairshill,
    I hear fond welcome tones,—
Sae I will sing o' Mary's skill,
    Her matchless milk and scones.

I've dined wi' Lairds o' micht and means,
    Wi' Factors I've been fou';
Hae Provosts, Baillies, 'mang my frien's
    And Ministers anew :
I've kissed and coortit maidens fair,
    Confab'd wi' learned dons ;
But a' sic joys will ne'er compare
    Wi' Mary's milk and scones.

Now let me whisper in your ear—
    But this ye mauna tell—
Tho' Mary's skill to me is dear,
    I like her some hersel';
That winsome face—that modest grace—
    For gowd and gear atones,
Sae fill your glass, drink to the lass
    That bakes the Lairshill scones.

INTRODUCTORY ADDRESS,

SPOKEN BY MISS ANNIE BALDWIN,

HER MAJESTY'S OPERA HOUSE, JUNE, 1880.

LADIES AND GENTLEMEN,—
"Welcome the coming, speed the parting guest"—
A golden rule in homely terms exprest;
How fondly do I hope such "claim of right"
May prove sure talisman for me to-night;
A charm to aid my simple, earnest words
As now I plead acceptance on these boards—
Acceptance here, within each generous heart
That loves the Drama and the Actor's art.
Your gracious smiles set half my fears at rest—
Pray may I deem myself "a welcome guest?"

These faltering lines of introduction spoken,
I gladly hold the ice between us broken,
And, warming to my work, proceed to say
How I the part of Hostess mean to play.

(But here I maunna craw owre croose,
'Tis serious business takin' up a hoose;
Yet naething venture ye can naething gain—
A' women like a fireside o' their ain.
Forgive my Scotch tho' scarcely pure or thorough;
Yet I have been *The Witch of Edinboro!*)

We players share but scanty steadfast joys—
Spoiled, petted, scorned, like children with their toys,
So as a "wandering star" I cease to roam,
And make this northern sphere my chosen home—

A home to which I heartly invite you
With fixed intent to humour and delight you :
Sit where you please, in that I ask no voice—
"You pays your money and you takes your choice."
    And now, methinks, I hear some patron hint—
"Your programme, Madam Hostess, pray present,
Give us the cue." Well, sir,.of course I mean
To signalise my sway in Aberdeen
By potent acts, to please both grave and gay—
Through "tales oft told"—stage pictures of the day ;
Shakespere and kin must, king-like, grace our bills,
While Robertson, with Byron, Harvey, Wills,
Shall yield fresh mental fare—strong, caustic, light,
Set fitly forth—judge by our start to-night.
Music, be sure, will grant rich store of pleasure—
Parisian movements—England's comelier measure.
Fair, pleasant fruit the summer eves will bring—
Our autumn hours may hear "Les Cloches" ring ;
Then heavier staple on to Christmas time,
When, presto ! change to gorgeous Pantomime.
    Next, what of stars ? some longing soul may ask.
Well, frankly, 'tis no easy, hopeful task
To catch theatric orbs of "light and leading"—
The mighty dollar our front rank is weeding ;
But I may mention, I shall make a rule
To draw this way both Sullivan and Toole.
Ah ! how I'd joy to mark you thrill, weep, cower
Beneath the spell of Henry Irving's power.
So trust me—trust an earnest woman's wit,—
Here you have cause to prize such influence yet ;
Proud shall I be if I can justly claim
Such love as clings round Mrs. Pollock's name.

"Welcome the coming, speed the parting guest :
Yes, there I'll close and let you guess the rest.
And yet, before these greeting lines take end,
Just one kind word to our way-going friend—
To him whose ruling, managerial wand
Must now be held by my less practised hand ;
Where'er his lot, doubt not but memory's chord
Will leally wake at thought of Bon-Accord—
My chosen home—for his he goes in quest ;
You've welcomed me, so "speed the parting guest."
       Thus ends scene first in my new Lessee life—
Keep now your plaudits for
                    "THE WORKMAN'S WIFE."

A VAGRANT VALENTINE.

O blessings on ye, Lilian dear,
   Fond blessing on ye fa';
For I have watch'd your smile, your tear,
   Unseen, unkent by a':
The wealth o' joy that has been mine,
When I hae pressed my lips to thine,
Shall round this heart aye closely twine
     Till life's cord breaks, my Lilian.

Last night, alone, my Lilian dear,
   Ye lay upon my breast;
And whispered words 'twas heav'n to hear,
   Your secret love confest:
O treasured ever be the hour
When passion held us in its power,
Earth hath for me no richer dower,
     Then thy soul's truth, my Lilian.

When years have flown, my Lilian dear,
   And this poor hand is cold;
When other eyes your smiles may cheer,
   And other arms enfold,—
Perchance as evening shadows fall,
And memory past times will recall,
Thou'lt think of one you said was all—
     Yes, all the world to thee, Lilian.

BRIDAL SONG

CONTRIBUTED FROM THE PRESS TABLE AT MARRIAGE OF THE

PRINCESS ROYAL, BALMORAL, 1858.

While gaily proud City bells ring bridal chimes,
And laureates and minstrels in sweet flowing rhymes
    Sing welcome and greeting to this festal day :
Here far 'mid our Highland hills join we the strain,
While loud-pealing pibrochs take up the refrain,
Shouting—joy to thy daughter, fair Queen of our Isles,
May her path, like thine own, be encircled with smiles—
    Her presence a blessing, and gentle her sway.

What though no rich splendour, no pageant be here,
Though deep frowns the corrie, wild boundeth the deer,
    And "dark Lochnagar" clad in snow gloometh grey :
Yet mark ye yon beacon fires gleaming afar,
From lofty Craig-gowan to rocky Braemar ;
O ! these are *our* love-lights ; the quaich and the horn
The goblets we drain to thee—England's first-born,
    And joyously hail we thy blithe bridal day.

Although never more may our valley rejoice
At the fall of thy footstep, the sound of thy voice,
    And thy coming be welcomed by dowie and gay :
Yet often thy thoughts may in after years roam
To the scene of thy life's-morn—thy loved Highland home ;
And true shall our hearts beat to thee and to thine,
While the Dee runs its course, or Craig Nich rears a pine,
    And fondly we'll cherish this blithe bridal day.

MY NEIGHBOUR THE MILLER.

My neighbour the Miller has muscle and girth,
  His foot tak's the grun' like the dunt o' a hammer;
His laugh soons like music, leal soul-heezing mirth,
  His word comes fair-furth-the-gait, nae halt nor stammer.
A chip o' langsyne, he prefers grog to wine,
  An oxter pouch lined weel wi' honest won siller,
Frae Fittie to Fife, I wad lay ye my life—
  There's nae truer man than my neighbour the Miller.

When the mill wheel is silent, the water at rest,
  My frien' fills his pipe, treasured joy, to content him;
Sits 'neath his ain fig-tree, like saint pure and blest,
  At peace wi' the warl, pleased wi' what Fate hath sent him.
When at Market or Fair, ye'll fin' nane trusted mair,
  In the Kirk he's a power as a ne'er failing pillar;
To anger full slow—kind to age, want or woe,—
  There's a big human heart in my neighbour the Miller.

He's fond o' a cronie to join in a rubber,
  Can share a safe tumbler, and loes a bit sang;
Tho' still at his table-heid wise-like and sober—
  Yet under his shadow nicht never grows lang.
Roun' his blithesome fireside,—tender father and guide;
  His wife, happy helpmate, he's aye bringin' till her;
While seed time and rain gladden ploo-land and plain,
  He hopes and looks heaven-ward my neighbour the Miller.

PROLOGUE

Spoken by Mr. A. McNeill, Manager, Aberdeen Theatre Royal, at Performance given in the Music Hall, by the Volunteers, for the benefit of a comrade who, passing safely as a soldier through the Indian Mutiny, lost his arm on resuming work at a local foundry, 1865.

LADIES AND GENTLEMEN,—
                     I, a humble player,
Whose chosen task is setting brain-wrought mimic fare
In varied form and dress before your ears and eyes,
Assuming many parts to teach, warn, and surprise
Through aid of tinsel show, stage trick, and maskéd plaint
Venture, with diffidence, *sans* powder, patch, or paint,
A character quite new—though strict in keeping here—
I come a self-enlisted, loyal Volunteer—
A Volunteer sent forward with a flag of truce
The aim and actors of the night to introduce.

    Ah me ! how much I miss the well-known "sets" and scenes,
The splendid airy castles ! canvas forest greens !
The ever-blooming groves ! the halls of dazzling light !
With beings always young, fair, beautiful, and bright !
The Green-room hints, "the wings," the watchful Prompter's cue—
Of these I'm all bereft, and so must trust to you
To bear with me, while for my friends behind
I crave you'll "to their failings be a little blind."
    And yet why should they doubtful either fear or pause !
Have they not half the battle with them in their cause?
They ask not for themselves—a comrade in his need,
His is the oar they pull, and *his* the boat they speed ;

Lend them your cheering smiles, then with that favouring gale
The wished-for haven's sure : there's no such word as fail.

My gentle Ladies list, and soon thou wilt surrender,
The flag of truce I bear has motto True and Tender.
Good Gentlemen, your ears—the terms I will propose
Would earn capitulation from the sternest foes.
My story's noble, sad : a broken sword in sheath :
The soldier's courted lot ! alas ! no soldier's wreath.

Look back across the path of time for seven peaceful years,
And see our weeping country bathed in vain soul-sickening tears :
Look back, and wander tremblingly o'er India's ravished clime,
And mourn the reign of mutiny—its horrors and its crime :
Look back, and shuddering think upon dark Cawnpore and its
    well—
No bloodier page of history our annals ere may tell—
Look back, and sigh for helpless babe and loving mother's fate,
Then give the meed of glory due th' unconquered "Seventy-Eight :"
Look back, at Lucknow's longing ones—their all undaunted stand,
Then follow, as your hearts beat high, that little kilted band :
Look back, and watch like forlorn hope old Scotland's tartans
    stream,
The bagpipes' challenge ringing shrill--the ready claymores' gleam :
Look back, and join, as join ye would, upon their matchless march,
Those shot nor shell can halt nor pale, no noon-tide heat may parch :
Look back, ye see them day by day go fighting inch by inch.
No arm grows weary of the fray, no sleepless eye doth flinch :
Look back, to find one conflict close when sinks the evening sun—
Look back, and when the morning wakes another strife's begun :
Look back, and hail them hastening on to succour and to save—
Grey Havelock's bearded Highlanders, the bravest of the brave !

Our comrade's tale is well nigh told.   Of that leal kilted band
Who shed a halo ne'er to fade upon their native land,—

Who from the first dread warning flash until the flame burnt done,
Ne'er uttered plaint or thought of self—*he* of that few was one;
And one and all were heroes there, as Europe wide confess'd,
Both those who stood and those who fell—all hallowed be their rest!

When India's soil again was ours, and "wild war's blast was
    blawn,"
When from a grim and gory night joy brought a gladsome dawn,
Our comrade leaned upon his arms and welcomed blood's surcease,
Sought home and friends, put past the sword and joined the ranks
    of peace:
Yet—such Life's all uncertain lot—though spared by shot and shell,
Amongst the shafts of Industry our gallant comrade fell!

My duty's done. My mates plead not with faint and abject
    whine—
They fight for one who in sore strait fought well for their's—and
    thine.
Then in their generous sport to-night excuse slight specks and flaws,
Be not too critical, I pray, look at them through their cause.
That noble cause as Volunteers your sympathy commands,
So as they justly have your hearts—why, do not spare your hands!

WITH THE FLEET—1878.

Come, lads, and listen to a stave—
  Our ship goes softly slow—
There's scarce a ripple on the wave,
  No sound above—below.
Our Captain reads, as from a book,
  Yon message hoisted high,
There's longing in his eager look,
  And dare-do in his eye.

      Perchance this stillness doth forewarn
        The brewing of the blast,
      And then, mates, this must be our yarn—
        "Nail colours to the mast.'

'Tis silent all on sea and shore,
  But fancy, weaving spells,
Brings, echo-like, the ocean o'er
  The chime of Sabbath bells :
And psalms we sung, with holy words
  Of youth's bright sunny days,
Come back again on memory's chords,
  To chasten manhood's ways.

      But, mates, this stillness may forewarn
        The brewing of the blast,
      And, then, good-bye to song and yarn—
        "Nail colours to the mast."

We leave fine talk and jawing fuss
　To wiser heads than ours ;
We bear no grudge to Turk or Russ,
　Or t' other stuck-up Powers.
But if there's fighting—friends or foes—
　We claim what's right and fair ;
We don't much care what tack it blows,
　Just let us have our share.

　　So, if this stillness should forewarn
　　　The brewing of the blast,
　　Why, then, mates, pass the good old yarn—
　　　" Nail colours to the mast."

MY PRINCESS OF THE HILL.

Come genial Spring with bud and bloom, come with thy strength-
    ening breeze,
Come with new verdure to the field, fresh leaflet to the trees ;
My soul exults with glad delight to hail thy lengthening day,—
My spirit warms with ardent glow—even as a boy at play :
My heart beats fast and fondly with manhood's noblest thrill—
In thought I'm in the presence of my Princess of the Hill.

'Twas on a bleak November day when first I felt her spell,
I walked beside her wonder-struck, strange silence o'er me fell ;
All nature looked so bare and blank, a chill was in the air,
But 'neath her smile the sodden ground, the barren bush, grew fair ;
That graceful form, those soft low tones, worked with enchantress
    skill,—
Earth even as I her influence owned—my Princess of the Hill.

Ah me ! how poor a thing am I this lady's love to win,
A weary brain-tasked labourer 'mid worldly strife and sin ;
Whilst she a being of purer sphere moves stately as a queen—
With radiant face and lustrous eyes all star-like in their sheen :
I dreamt I might but worship her, admire and gaze my fill—
But joy ! she deigned to smile on me, my Princess of the Hill.

O, kind hath been her gracious ways, and passing sweet her words ;
A whisper—and my willing ear rings with harmonious chords ;
A pressure of her soft white hand—my heart's blood runneth fast ;
A kiss, a swift and rose-flush kiss—'tis bliss too great to last :
I look not into Fate's dread book, but Future have thy will—
No shadows cloud our bye-gone hours,—my Princess of the Hill.

I know not if Love's alchemy beguiles the gazer's eye
And makes the flower of yester-eve to-day of rarer dye ;
Yet this I vow my lady's face more beautiful doth grow—
Her sylph-like form more perfect still—more radiant bright her
    brow :
Is this Love's raptured limner power ?—nay, look ! she doth fulfil
Far more than feeble pen may trace—my Princess of the Hill.

There's a glory in the summer morn,—a paradise in flowers,—
There's happiness to each and all in this changeful world of ours ;
The true heart ever trusteth with a strength no blow may rend—
So fond memories abiding will cheer me to the end.
Speed on swift Time but in your flight leave, leave unbroken still
The chain that binds this soul to hers—my Princess of the Hill.

ADDRESS

SPOKEN BY MR. JAMES R. GIBSON, LEADING ACTOR, ON HIS
BENEFIT NIGHT, THEATRE ROYAL, ABERDEEN, 1873.

[The Play had been " Rob Roy." The House crowded.
As curtain falls the Baillie steps to front.]

My conscience ! Helen ? Rab ? They a' are gane,
And left the Baillie, blatelike, here alane !
I'm in a swither : sall I rin or bide ?
There's nae place hereaboot whaur ane micht hide,
Nae open door, a press, or handy lum—
　　　　　[Speaking to ancient member of the orchestra.
Man, ye micht stow's awa' within your drum !
He shaks his heid : na, that cock winna fecht !
And I'm in sair distress wi' doonricht fricht.
A Baillie feart !　There's nae man here my foe ?
Sall I then, coor'd like, flee ?　My conscience—no !
　　　　[Taking off wig, etc., and advancing to foot-lights.

LADIES AND GENTLEMEN,—

With the Poet and the Painter, ye have lingered o'er " Langsyne,"
While the Actor lent his meed of Art, and Music—gift divine—
Made melody with voice and string to win the willing ear,
To stir the sympathetic soul, and wake responsive tear;
Ye have followed at the Wizard's call by mountain, lake, and stream,
Till in fancy 'neath his conjuring there passed a living dream—
A vanish'd page of olden days, but ah ! how potent still
To fan the flame in Scottish breast that time nor change can chill :

Then while the charm of plaid and pipe, the tartan, snood, and
　　plume
Hangs round ye, like an incense sweet of heath and hill perfume—
While yet these feelings pulse and sway—Pardon if I intrude
To offer—not as Actor now—a full heart's gratitude.

No : not the mime or actor, it is the man would speak,
If fitting words might form and flow, though words indeed are weak
To utter half the debt of thanks I at your feet could lay :
The heart is rich in eloquence—the lips but poor to pay.

Not now as Mountebank or King—-*Belphegor* or *Macbeth*—
I conjure with the ball and bowl, do battle to the death ;
Not now as *Melnotte, Romeo,* I dream of naught but love,
Rave of "sweet orange groves, soft lutes," and "kiss my lady's
　　glove ; "
Not now as auld *John Howieson,* I rescue good King James,
And " fin mysel' clean oot o' breath " 'mang courtly knights and
　　dames ;
Not now I woo leal Jeannie Deans, as pauky *Dumbiedykes,*
Or brag wi' *Dandie Dinmont* o' his terriers and his tykes;
Not now doon Glasgow Gallowgate, wi' Mattie I step gaily,
A portrait from langsyne re-framed, "a hale Sautmarket Baillie."
The tinsel, paint, and spangles, the trappings of my art,
From these I borrow touch nor trick to aid my present part,
That part the man's true character—Pardon, nor deem me rude,
In offering—not as Actor now—a full heart's gratitude.

I look up into your faces with a pleased and proud surprise,
I can see a wealth of kindness beaming from your generous eyes ;
My ears drink in with eager joy your hand and voice acclaim—
And I feel I'm not unworthy all to bear the honoured name
Of true-born son of Bon-Accord—for dear, aye dear to me
Is the ever brave and comely—" Silver City by the Sea."

Ah ! oft, my friends, when wandering far, fond thought would
    yearning roam
Pack to the scenes of early days, my own belovéd home,
And when the fight was hard and long, when Faith's lamp flicker'd
    low,
When the future seemed an emptiness, Fortune a jealous foe,
Some pitying angel whispered me—"Still onward, upward press!"—
Then Hope's bright star arose and shone upon a night like *this!*
                                [*The Prompter's bell rings.*
    The Prompter calls : And this his cue—"No longer, sir, intrude,
To offer such poor tribute of a full heart's gratitude."

    Then, friends, adieu !   Whate'er my fate, whate'er my lot may be,
There's nought can rend my longings from "the City by the Sea."
And when I dare forget this scene—the halo it hath flung
About my path—then I'll forget my ain auld mither tongue.
The road to fame the Actor treads is a steep and slippery brae,
But your voices like a trumpet shall herald me on the way ;
By thee to-night I feel love's might girt round me as a sword,
To strive, wait, serve—soul, brain and nerve—for home, for Bon-
    Accord.

WICKET, BAT AND BALL.

(Air: Lass of Richmond Hill).

O ! Dick may gaily hunt his hounds,
   And Jack set sail for sea :
While soldier Ralph courts fame and wounds,
   Bill loves the forest free ;
Let Jack, Dick, Bill, rove at their will,
   And brave Ralph proudly fall,
Their sport can ne'er with ours compare—
   The wicket, bat and ball.

     Chorus—The jolly bat and ball,
         The merry bat and ball,
     No sport say I, 'neath heaven's blue sky,
         Like wicket, bat and ball.

There's Ned he is an angler keen,—
   Tom boasts a rifle true :
Fred holds high " court " on tennis green,
   With Mabel, Maud and Prue.
Let Ned go fish, give Tom his wish,
   And soft Fred vow " loves-all,"—
We envy not their choice and lot,—
   Be ours the bat and ball.

     Chorus—The jolly bat and ball,
         The merry bat and ball,
     No sport say I, 'neath heaven's blue sky,
         Like wicket, bat and ball.

Then prosper aye our noble game,
 To none it e'er shall yield,
While we can cheerily chant its fame,
 And hit, guard, bowl or field :
'Gainst stump and bail, e'en age wont rail,
 Their pleasures never pall :
Strength, courage, youth—hope, patience, truth,
 Meet round the bat and ball.

> *Chorus*—The jolly bat and ball,
> The merry bat and ball,
> No sport say I, 'neath heaven's blue sky,
> Like wicket, bat and ball.

A MEMORY.

MARION—
 So dearly loved in blissful bye-gone years,
   Here lone to-night, with reverent sorrow bowed,
 I mourn thy fate with sad and silent tears,
   And fain would kiss thee in thy snowy shroud :
     But, ah ! it may not be—
 Ne'er shall again mine eyes that sweet face see.

MARION—
 Although our paths for long have lain apart,
   And word nor look hath passed us twain between,
 Yet thou belov'd hast held within my heart
   A sacred place, a memory ever green :
     But now the shadow falls,
 Life's Eventide hath come : The Master calls.

MARION—
 To-morrow they will lay thee in thy grave,
   And o'er thee will be placed a wreath of flowers,
 But none may know the grateful hand that gave
   Such offering meet of unforgotten hours :
     Nor lips nor pen may tell
 Of what hath been. Marion, pure-souled, Farewell !

KATE O' KIRKHILL.

" The gloomy night was gathering fast,"—say at Nigg!

Witches and fairies,—Fairies and witches,
  Beings o' flesh and blood, imps i' the air ;
Coupin' Hope's cairt now 'mang daisies, now ditches,
  Atween ye, heaven help us ! come canker and care.
Through glamour and glances ye whiles drive me doitet,
  At times 'tis conjectured, I'm past doctor's skill ;
My cronies they hint, I think nae shame to write it,
  I've saftnin' o' brain aboot Kate o' Kirkhill.

Witches and fairies,—Fairies and witches,
  Wills-o'-the-wisp,—mortals steadfast as truth ;
Some trachel'd and auld ridin' broomsticks and crutches,—
  And mony o' Angel mould, golden wi' youth.
Jist tell me, my brither, if ne'er in your bosom
  Ye fand the fond jaggin o' Love's fiery thrill ?
If ye did, then ye'll ken hoo I shun a' that's gruesome
  To live in the sunshine o' Kate o' Kirkhill.

Witches and fairies,—Fairies and witches,
  Ah ! why will ye no lat a trustin' soul be ?
I carena' for honours, I crave fame nor riches,—
  Content is the dower far dearer to me.
O ! love leave your hame by the wild beatin' ocean,—
  My heart like the sobbin' waves ne'er can be still ;
Come end wi' ae' laigh word this weary commotion,—
  Jist say you're my ain,—my sweet Kate o' Kirkhill.

To J. T.

"A friend of mine in his journey."—St. Luke.

Go on thy way.   Tread the appointed path,
And own, by sea and land, what love the Father hath.

Be of good cheer : let hope inspire thy breast ;
Even as thy days thy strength shall be,—then cometh rest.

Fear not nor doubt : fond hearts will faithful be,
And love, with old time sway, unseen encircle thee.

For thee afar fair flowers, unborn, shall spring,
Bright bows of promise break, and birds new carols sing.

Keep summer in thy soul.   We part to meet
Here or—the Master calling—near the mercy seat.

Then forward friend.   Trust in the coming day ;
Heav'n's gifts are manifold.   Farewell.   Go on thy way.

"SCENE IN THE CIRCLE,"

WRITTEN FOR THE BENEFIT NIGHT OF A FAVOURITE CIRCUS JESTER.

The Jester is leaving the Circle when the Ring Master speaks:—

Why, Seal, it strikes me you might air your wit
By offering thanks for this rare benefit?

Jester—Give thanks ! Ah yes, if words could but express
The feeling born of this night's happiness
Quick to my lips with welling joy would start
Thanksgiving tribute from a grateful heart.

Ring Master—Bravo ! good fool : you've struck the key for sermon
or for song,
Proceed, your friends will listen,—only don't spin out *too* long.

Jester—" Good fool," you say : the character I fondly try to earn
From gentle folks, and simple folks, from grey-beard and from
bairn.
A moment's space then grant me, while in words, poor, but
sincere,
I strive to thank all round and round for their welcome presence
here.

LADIES AND GENTLEMEN,
There's an old story of an Eastern Prince,
Who lived,—I really know not how long since,—
But he was robed in gold, and moved in wondrous state,
Beauty knelt at his feet, tried warriors kept his gate ;
Both far and near, alike by land and sea,
His word was law,—so great a Prince was he.

F

Obedience was his due,—yet all in vain he strove
To touch one human heart, or wake one smile of love.
To him no voice for friend or foe e'er sued,—
He felt not, proved not, won not Gratitude,
So when this monarch died his own Court Jester's wit
Took form of epitaph and thus he gravely writ :—

> *Dust rest in dust: below this stone is laid*
> *A Prince who lived, a Prince who now is dead;*
> *He ruled unloved,—unwept he passed away:*
> *The curtain's down ; each dog must have his day.*
> *Reader in silence muse, this history is ended:*
> *The less that's said,—the sooner 'twill be mended.*

Ring Master—A shrewd fool that,—sarcastic too, I wean,
    But tell me pray, what doth the riddle mean ?
Jester—Ay, there's the rub ! Perchance not much—one of those
    quips and cranks
    On which I, fool like, find a peg to hang my humble thanks ;
    For, Sir, were I of regal rank, a Sultan, Czar, or King,
    My sceptre power should be displayed within this magic ring,
    My motley dress as medicine should wake the dullest brain,
    "Laugh and be happy all who may," prescription, wholesome,
    plain.
    Gay cheerfulness should spread around till with conceit and jest
    I'd make each fair maid's temper, the sweetest, gentlest, best !
    Young men should wooing go with speed, and prove so kind
    and true
    That 'midst the flowers of wedded bliss, there nought could be
    of rue !
    Yes, quite a wealth of marriages the Parsons would proclaim,
    The stakes being now but "two-and-six," at that engaging
    game !

Thus would I reign and ever prize my generous patron's weal,
While 'gainst Church strife, Town Council tiffs I'd set my
  hand and Seal !
    So ends my little story, and now to all Good Night !
Houp la ! the Queen of Beauty comes to take her aerial flight,
Music, brave minstrels, music ! hark to the entrance bell !
Houp la ! again,—Ring Master thanks, yea, thanks and fond
  Farewell.

"PEACE OFFERINGS."

Thanks Eldra for your flowers.   Though withered, cold and broken
  They breathe to me thoughts tender, true and warm ;
Lifeless and odour-dead, yet are they welcome token,
  Old times and feelings still have power to charm,—
That in thy nobler word when thine own self thou art,
  Hope, trust and ruth, enduring, simple, free,
Hold rule and triumph in thy generous heart,
  And I am sharer in their victory.

"Peace offerings," ye say.   Dearer to me as such
  Than jewelled gift, or far brought costly gem :
Of this world's rusting wealth my store can ne'er be much,—
  Yet I have some rare treasures, and 'mongst them
Hereafter when I reckon up what most I prize,
  These wasted violets, all scentless though they be,
Shall yield the grateful joy that changeth not nor dies—
  The memory of moments spent with thee.

Ye smile at this my verse.   Ye know me all unread
  In floral lore.   Not mine the wit or spell
Twinned lovers fondly fancy lurk in bud and blade—
  And yet, methinks, I should interpret well
The secret of these leaves,—a secret tho' unspoken
  In silence eloquent to me of happy hours :
"Peace offerings," ye say :   A peace ne'er to be broken
  By unkind word again.   Thanks Eldra for your flowers.

A CRICKET LAY.

To J. A. A. in the Book of the Aberdeenshire Cricket Club Bazaar, 1888.

"A bit of rhyme for your Bazaar?"—why, certainly, here goes—
Tho' let me tell you in my time they didn't have such shows;
But then things alter, and folks must go moving quick along—
"Keep to the right!" is now the cry, and do not stop the throng.
Yet some things, Jack, know little change, aye ready! is the ticket,
And patience, temper, fair play, pluck, are watchwords still at
    Cricket.

You'd like to hear about the Elevens—the cracks of my young days?
Ah! sir, they're scattered far and wide, who then won willow-bays—
'Tis an innings over two score years since first I watched the bails,
But yet you know of early joys fond memory rarely fails—
So looking in my fire to-night I see a crowd of faces,
A picture, Jack, in miniature, of the Broadhill at the races.

We had not daily broad-sheets then, nor telegraphic wire,
To give the tip from London straight who stood the Champion shire—
'Twas oft a week before we heard from the "Oval" or from
    "Lord's"—
What now you read at any hour on big newspaper boards.
No picked Australian teams came o'er to fright our English players
With "demon" Spofforth funking fits, or "terror" Turner scares!

But don't mistake! you must not think there were no giants then,
To count with Grace, Reid, Lohmann, Wood, and other first-class
    men—
Why, there was good old Fuller Pilch, for "centuries" in he went—
(He was only a working tailor, sir, *but* also "Lion of Kent.")
Stout Alfred Mynn, Box, Felix, old Lilywhite, and Clarke,
Then Wisden, Tarrant, Lockwood—Myres, Chatterton, and Dark.

But now mayhaps you'd like a word about my own kind mates,
Who used to gather on the Links—we nothing knew of "gates"—
Ah ! sir, you bring back halcyon days, and touch a tender theme
I can see them rising one by one here through my fireside dream—
But few remain of that far time, they greet old friends no more,
Their "silver city by the sea" is now yon "golden shore."

Well, Jack, that was a minor touch—so again the major key,—
For Auld Lang Syne rings in my ear—I watch them in their glee—
There's Nisbet with his twister lobs—then Alick Watt's full pitch—
And Brown whose swinging swipes meant 6, to the Bannermill
      dyke ditch,
Jim Forbes of the horny hand, who never missed a catch—
And Miller who from hottest fire drew many a doubtful match.

Dear Davie Duguid, deaf but sure, the prince of all our bowlers,
Z, who never *could* be out—you always get some growlers—
The Walkers, Playfair, Nornable—Pape, Mitchell, Riddell, Allan—
(A very king of bankers, Jack, and Melbourne is his dwallin',)
Bob Maitland, handsome Gosden, of medicals the swell—
His batting was a study, and the ladies loved him well.

And what about yourself? you ask: well, they dubbed me, fact,
      "Hawk-eye,"
My post was "slip," because, you see, I was no good to "shy"—
But a warrior bold I was to block, a Bannerman to stay,
The slow game of this ancient child it wouldn't do to-day—
Still runs are runs, got how or where, in singles or in lumps,
And if you double figures mean, why, you must mind your stumps.

But look, hurrah ! the tartans come, the Barracks' choice Eleven,
Amongst them Knights and Honourables—first number, yes, a "7,"
Lord William Russell captained them—stood point close to the
      wicket,
A soldier frank, cared not for caste, liked all who played true cricket,

With courtly Captain Chichester, tall Ensign Brickenden—
On Alma's height, in after years, they won their spurs like men.

Of later times and fresher hands, 'tis not for me to tell :
You've been, Jack, in the thick of it and know the "talent" well.
Look round the Ground Pavilion Wall, and mark the roll-call there
Of those we're proud to honour, in whose victories we share ;
Yet if these lines should see the light as record of the game,
Let the printer choose his biggest type when setting LUMSDEN'S
  name.

And so I end this rambling rhyme with "Success to the Bazaar,"
And lift my cap to Cricketers here, near us, or afar,
It makes not what their calling is—sword, hammer, pen, or file,
Whether they live by sweat of brow or boast an honest "pile,"
Be this their maxim o'er the world whatever may befall—
Boys, always keep an upright bat and a sure eye on the ball.

THE FLOWING CATARRH.

*Apologetic Postscript read by President Smith-Shand, at the
Centenary Dinner of Aberdeen Medico-Chirurgical
Society, 14th December, 1889.*

When the cold of December comes freezing,
　　With the morning sharp, bracing, and clear ;
When by night you are snifting and sneezing,
　　And your eye yields the unbidden tear—
Why, then, don your cosiest linder,
　　See no window or door stands ajar,
Get hot water and double the " cinder "—
　　And sing hey ! for a flowing Catarrh !

When a chill creeps the whole body over,
　　And anon you're at high fever heat ;
When to send for the Doctor you hover,
　　And muse what he'll give you to eat ;
Then your thoughts conjure up a vile mixture,
　　With a taste between " castor " and tar,
So you vote—Stay at home like a fixture
　　And nurse your free-flowing Catarrh.

The Medicos form a great faction—
　　Chirurgery—noble, of course ;
And a hundred full years of their action—
　　Well—the world might be better or worse :
So I waft you, Sir Chairman, a greeting—
　　May no " sends for " your dinner joys mar,—
Here's success to your cent'nary meeting—
　　While I treat my free-flowing Catarrh !

THE FARMER'S LIFE.

(With Old English Refrain).

The farmer leads a kingly life true monarch of the field;
By day and night the generous earth to him doth tribute yield;
The Summer, Autumn, Winter, Spring, bring mercies ever new,—
     " Singing wo! my lads, gee wo!
     Drive on my boys, hi, ho!"
O! who could live a nobler life than happy farmers do?

In Spring the quickened verdure peeps from the teeming soil—
Each tender leaf and opening bud rewards the sower's toil
He watcheth well their gentle growth nursed by the rain and dew,—
     "And sings wo! my lads gee wo!
     Drive on my boys, hi, ho!"
Say, who could live a nobler life than happy farmers do?

When Summer, in full glory, reigneth o'er the gladsome earth,
The tuneful birds and nodding flowers make melody and mirth;
The farmer marks the ripening corn put on its harvest hue,—
     "And sings wo! my lads gee wo!
     Drive on my boys, hi, ho!"
Yea, none may lead a nobler life than happy farmers do.

See Autumn lovely Autumn now her richest robes unfold,
And smiling plenty waving wide in ranks of gleaming gold,
Then grateful hearts o'erflow with love for blessings rare nor few,—
     " Singing wo! my lads gee wo!
     Drive on my boys, hi, ho!"
O! who could live a nobler life than happy farmers do?

When Winter rules, the furrowed land rests 'neath the freshning snow,
The farmers ingle brightly then sends forth a welcome glow;
He joys to see around his hearth friends and companions true,—
　　"And sings wo! my lads gee wo;
　　Drive on my boys, hi, ho!"
None, none may live a nobler life than happy farmers do!

"W. S."

*Lines accompanying Portrait of the Right Reverend Monsignor
Stopani in Book of Grand Indian Bazaar,
December, 1890.*

In gloomy narrow lane, in stirring wide-spread street—
See him with earnest face, and never-tiring feet.

The light, swift, welcome step; the frank, sweet, ready smile;
His heart upon his sleeve, a nature free of wile.

List, as in tender accents he entreats his flock,
To cling unto the Cross, and build upon the Rock.

Mark, how with outstretched hand he meets the poor, opprest,
And gently guides the young in ways of truth and rest.

Priest, Preacher, to his own, in verity and deed;
Friend, Citizen, beloved of every sect and creed.

Speed, faithful servant, on; brave messenger of peace:
The Master's business thine—thine that it yield increase.

ADDRESS

SPOKEN BY MR. JOHN CAVANAH, GENERAL MANAGER, HER

MAJESTY'S THEATRE, ABERDEEN, ON HIS BENEFIT

NIGHT, 9th JUNE, 1890.

LADIES AND GENTLEMEN,—

Although 'tis not according to my general use and wont
To face you o'er the footlights, my "stage-land" being in front,
Yet at your kind indulgent call I venture on the boards
To offer you my grateful thanks in few but earnest words.

Three years ago a hopeful friend, in phrase with good-will stored,
Said—"Try your fortune in the North, try brave old Bon-Accord,
The heads are hard, the granite too, but folks there have a way
Of keeping good things they may get—the chance is *you* will stay.'

The prophecy, I gladly own, in this case has proved right;
I do not seem a stranger now—witness the house to-night;
Leal, generous friends, with welcome warm, on every side I've met,
And memory will be tenantless when I your deeds forget.
Not mine the ready speaker's gift, not mine the writer's skill—
I would be eloquent indeed, if the lips obeyed the will;
Could the full, silent heart take voice—if feeling might have sway,
My gratitude in "flower of speech" would blossom like the May;
My thanks should fall upon your ears on this fair eve in June,
As loesome as "a melody that's sweetly played in tune."

Pardon weak words.   I've said enough : Yes, there we all agree;
Just let me add, before we part, I'm very pleased to see
So many of the Order gathered round me here to-night—
Their's is the "mystic tie" that keeps a brother's burden light.

And you my loyal patrons who with chorus, shout and song
Unite to help our mimic sport so tunefully along—
How like, how generous 'tis of you to rest from Student toil,
And for a moment cease to burn the midnight "grinding" oil!
Bright, prosperous, be your coming years—be leaders in the van
Of right 'gainst might, and proudly bear the badge of Gentleman.

Adieu. Once more I proffer all my thanks, devoted, true,
Your kindness long shall hold my heart. Adieu, again, Adieu.

THE QUEER CARLE.

A Carle cam' to the auld Laird's door,
He played Scots springs mair than a score,
He liltit strains o' youth and yore,
    And deftly changed the key :
His music breathed o' hills and howes,
Whaur Dee, the Don, and Ythan rows,
O' battle fields and fairy knowes
    Seen far aff Benachie.

We set him by the ingle neuk—
The lads forgot dam-brod and book,
The lasses roon him a' did jouk,
    He sang sae winningly :
He pettit Mary 'neath the chin,
Jean couldna' wyve nor Lizzie spin,
Wee Ailie said 'twad be nae sin,
    A kiss to him to gie.

The Laird, he heard the fiddle fine,
Thocht to himsel', but made nae sign,
Jist knacket's thooms oot-owre his wine,
    And set his wig a-jee ;
Bell vowed she saw him tak' the fleer,
Whan the Carle strak' up—"A wife wi' gear,"—
In dum'-show pairtner'd wi' his cheir,
    And danced richt merrily.

Neist week he lan'it at the Manse,
Sat cheek-for-chow wi' douce cook Nance,
Screwed up his pegs, and, as by chance,
                    Played "Whisky mak's gweed tea":
The Minister could write nae mair,
His dothers hearken'd on the stair,
Their mither froon'd, yet fain wad share
                    The blithesome revelry.

Oor deen Precenter, Jamie Yule,
He couldna' start his Singin' School—
'Tween Kirk o' Rayne and Folla-Rule—
                    The Carle kent *Do-Re-Mi!*
He filled the lateran for a raith,
He chantit hymns and anthems baith
At sic a rate folk hadna' breath,
                    Nor time, the words to see.

Whane'er 't got oot—The Carle is come!
The wabster left pirn, loom and thrum,
The tailor tired owre 's steeks to bum,
                    The sooter raxed his knee;
The blacksmith flang his hammer bye,
The herd loon hurriet hame his kye,
The vera' dogs wad crouchin' try,
                    To catch his kindly e'e.

By turns he crooned sae slow and sweet
O' frien's noo gane nae mair to meet,
That hearts in sympathy wad beat,
                    And tears come drappin free;
Then looder grew the swellin' chords,
The notes rang forth like clash o' swords—
"For Scotland onward! loons and lords,
                    And quit ye valiantlie."

He laid aff ballads, auld and new,
Queer stories tauld, some fause some true,
And far owre fest the hairst nichts flew
        Whan the Carle was in his glee.
But here nor there lang wad he bide,
Few tried to bleck, nane daured to guide,
There was a something,—wrath or pride,—
        Folk didna' care to dree.

On Saturdays, at broadest Meen,
Whan neighbour Dominies convene
To hae a rubber, weet their speen,
        And swap theology,
The Carle, aye a welcome guest,
Appeared, unfailin', in his best,
And took his place amang the rest,
        Whate'er the company.

On Kirk law, keen to cope wi' Pirie,
At reels, a match for Greig o' Garioch,
Even Bourtie's *Latin* he wad query
        By Melvin's verity ;
Owre Darwin's scheme he cautioned truce ;
Held views now vexin' Dods and Bruce,
And leuch 'boot some scribe playin' the deuce
        Wi' Eden's aipple tree !

Gane, gane alas ! that hope-bricht time
Whan hapless Smith was in his prime,
Then Tennyson, and homelier rhyme—
        Soul-stirring psalmody—
Would warm and win, be sung and read
Till some young hearts thocht what was said
Mair precious far than daily bread :—
        But that's a memory.

A bee in's bonnet ?   Mayhap twa',
We'll lat that flee stick to the wa',
The noblest wark has aye some flaw,—
             Herein is mystery :
His faith displayed the Poet's plan,—
Wi' him a man was still a man,
Whate'er his station, creed or clan,
             If stamped wi' honesty.

At length and last an Uncle deid,
Wha's gospel had through life been Greed ;
O' testament he left nae screed,
             Nor wife, nor bairn had he :
Oor Carle, coontin' next o' kin,
To acres rich and braid cam' in,
Ceased wanderin' ways and minstrel din,
             For County dignity.

Nae hungry man need pass his door,
He giveth freely of his store,
'Twas only lent him,—that, no more—
             A sacred trust in fee :
Then when the sun sinks in the west,
And shadows wrap Buck-Cabrach's crest,
The Carle, contented, dreams of rest,
             In a grave by Benachie.

DEE AND DON.

"Dee and Don shall run in one,"—
  So the olden fret foretells;
But till memory hath flown—
  While life's current ebbs and swells—
      Parted evermore to me
      Silent Don and silvery Dee.

Heart to heart must linkéd be,
  Joy and sorrow still to share,
Good with ill—'tis heaven's decree—
  Youth and age—the false, the fair—
      Pain and balm,—but smiles or tears
      Love endures even as the years.

Gadie, constant to the Don,
  Sighs farewell to Benachie;
Brawling Feugh o'er moor and stone,
  Sinks to rest in peaceful Dee:
      Sunder'd streams to ocean roll—
      Seek and find your destined goal.

Boyhood's day,—hope's golden prime,
  Hath a glory all its own,
Rich with melodies sublime,
  Heard for aye in undertone:
      Not to me till fades the sun
      "Dee and Don shall run in one."

ABERDEEN:

PRINTED BY LEWIS SMITH AND SON.

WAIFS OF RHYME—First Edition, pp. 62.

We have seldom met with racier bits of Scottish humour.—*Dundee Advertiser.*

The song, "The Plough," ought to be a Classic. THE WAIFS will meet a warm welcome in Northern homes.—*Banffshire Journal.*

Some of the Scotch Ballads remind us greatly of Allan Ramsay at his best. "Tam Teuchit" is instinct with the poetry of love and nature.—*Aberdeen Journal.*

There is no effort or elaboration in this Poet's strains. "Tam Teuchit's Reflections amang the Stooks" will live as long as the Scottish language.—*The British Weekly.*

The Dramatic Addresses written for high occasions at the "Old House in Marischal Street," will bring back pleasant memories. It is in the English and pathetic lyrics that the literary art of the writer is seen at its best.—*Aberdeen Free Press.*

Sixty-Fifth Thousand.

THE NORTHERN PSALTER AND HYMN TUNE BOOK,
Edited by WILLIAM CARNIE, Aberdeen.

Edited with great care and skill.—*Scotsman.*

Far and away the best book of its kind in Scotland for congregational worship.—*Perthshire Magazine.*

Without any reservation, we place "THE NORTHERN PSALTER" first amongst Scottish Collections.—*Dundee Advertiser.*

A treasure of Sacred Song that will stand comparison with any that has appeared in this country.—*Presbyterian Psalmodist.*

Nothing which the Aberdeen people have ever done, skilled as they are in Psalmody, can be compared with this collection of tunes.—*Fifeshire Journal.*

Will stand comparison with any collection published in the North since Edward Raban produced his "ABERDEEN PSALTER," nearly two centuries ago.—*Glasgow Daily Mail.*